THE TOTEM POLE

WITHDRAWN FROM STOCK

Alison Milford

Catherine Väse

For my special family in Canada
A.M.
To my dearest pal Fi-fi, Pablo and their
beautiful boy Temoc
C.V.

EGMONT
We bring stories to life

This edition published 2007 by Egmont UK Ltd
239 Kensington High Street, London W8 6SA
Text copyright © Alison Milford 2007
Illustrations copyright © Catherine Väse 2007
The author and illustrator have asserted their moral rights
ISBN 978 1 4052 3357 6
10 9 8 7 6 5 4 3 2 1
A CIP catalogue record for this title is available from the British Library.
Printed in Singapore.

Contents

Red Bananas

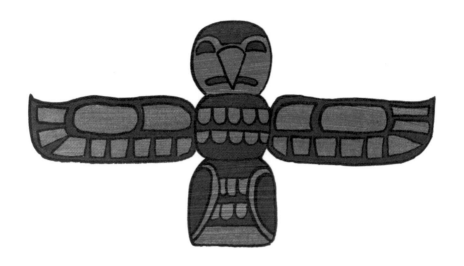

The Hole

'Gawu, why is there a big hole in the ground?' asked Kuna.

Gawu stopped carving a snake out of a stick and went to where his sister was standing. They both peered into the deep, dark hole.

'That's where our father's totem pole is going to be put up at the party tomorrow,' answered Gawu.

'Is it because he saved the chief's son from being attacked by a bear?' asked Kuna.

'Yes,' said Gawu proudly. 'He killed it with just one arrow.'

Two boys joined Gawu and Kuna.

'Your father is a true warrior!' said one of them. 'He is strong and brave.'

Your father is braver than you!

'To be a good Eagle warrior is very important. Don't you agree, Gawu?' smirked the second boy.

Gawu didn't answer. He rubbed the soft wood of his stick and carried on carving.

'One day, Gawu will also have a totem pole for being a strong and brave Eagle,' said Kuna proudly.

The two boys laughed nastily.

'Gawu will never be strong and brave. He's too busy carving bits of wood,' sneered one who looked as big as a horse. 'When I am older, I will be given a totem pole for being as strong as a moose.'

'That's nothing,' boasted the other boy, who looked as thin as a blade of grass.

'When I am older, I will be given a totem pole for running as fast as the wind.'

'When I am older I am going to carve the Eagle totem poles,' said Gawu.

'You have to be clever to be a totem pole carver!' exclaimed the thin boy. He snatched Gawu's carving. 'You can't even carve a worm!'

'It's not a worm, it's a snake!' shouted Gawu. He grabbed his carving back and ran off.

'Come back, Gawu,' called out Kuna. 'Where are you going?'

The Workshop

Gawu was going to the totem pole workshop. He loved to sit for hours watching Gulas, the wood carver, turn wood into wonderful shapes and creatures.

Gulas looked up from his carving as Gawu rushed in like a whirling tornado.

'What's the matter, Gawu?' he asked.

'I don't want to be strong and brave like

my father,' said Gawu angrily. 'I want to be a totem pole carver like you.'

'A carver also has to be strong and brave if he is to turn the great red cedar trees into totem poles,' said Gulas.

Gawu's eyes started to fill with tears.

'What do you think of the totem pole for your father?' said Gulas kindly.

Gawu looked at the tall, wooden pole. Covered in swirling patterns, colourful shapes and strange-looking creatures, it was one of the best totem poles he had ever seen.

'I have carved four creatures on it,' said Gulas. 'Do you know what they are?'

Gawu looked at the odd-looking creature staring at him from the bottom of the totem pole.

'You've carved a frog because it's as clever as my father,' replied Gawu. 'The next one is the bear because it's as brave and strong as my father.'

Gawu was not sure about the third creature. As he stroked its two wooden teeth, he suddenly remembered the animal who made dams in the nearby river.

'This must be the beaver,' he cried. 'It's wise and works hard just like my father!'

Gawu gasped when he saw the last creature. It looked so real.

You're so clever, Gulas.

At the top of the totem pole, perched a huge carved bird with enormous wings. All the totems of the Eagle tribe had one. The eagle was their special sign.

Gawu touched one of the eagle's feathers and was surprised to find it hard and cold.

'How did you make the feathers look so soft?' Gawu asked Gulas.

It looks so real!

'To be a good wood carver, you must first look at the wood. Is it long, short, straight, curvy, thin or thick?

Are there lines or marks on the wood? Next you must feel the wood. Is it smooth, rough, bumpy, hard, or soft? As you look and feel, you will start to see a shape or a creature appear in your mind. Then you can begin to carve, just like this.'

Gulas picked up his curved carving knife and began to carefully carve the eagle's talons.

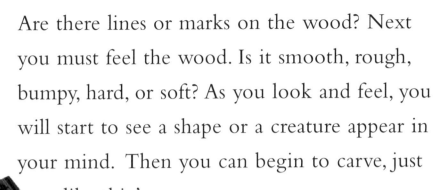

'Can I help you?' asked Gawu. 'I'm getting quite good at carving. Today, I carved a snake out of this stick! Look!'

Gawu tried to show Gulas his snake but Gulas did not look up from his work.

'To help me carve a totem pole, you will need to do a lot more than carve a simple snake out of an old stick!' said Gulas.

Gawu was just about to protest when

I must finish this.

Kuna walked by carrying a large, blue basket.

'There you are, Gawu!' she said. 'We have to go into the forest to pick berries.'

'I'm busy,' grumbled Gawu.

'Go, Gawu,' ordered Gulas. 'I need to get this totem pole finished.'

Gawu threw his carved snake away and stomped off towards the forest.

Come on, Gawu!

Rescue!

Gawu kicked the fallen leaves as he walked grumpily along the forest path.

'Hurry up, Gawu,' called Kuna as she ran deeper into the forest. 'I know where we can go.'

Gawu picked up a long, knobbly stick and hit a thorny bush in anger.

'Picking berries is girl's work,' he shouted

at the trees around him. 'All I want to do is carve!' he yelled as he hit the leaves of a tall cedar tree with his stick.

Gawu threw himself to the ground and started to draw the face of a bear in the earth with his stick.

Suddenly a frightened deer rushed by, making him jump.

'Kuna, are you there?' he called.

There was no answer.

'Kuna, where are you?' he shouted.

He listened for a sound but the forest had gone quiet.

Gawu felt cold.

Something was very wrong.

Gawu ran through the forest as fast as he could, using his stick to beat down the bushes. Suddenly he saw a glint of blue through the trees. It was Kuna's basket!

Quickly, he ran towards it. Then he stopped. There in front of him, frozen in terror, stood Kuna. Gawu followed her eyes and saw a large wolf prowling slowly towards her.

Gawu gulped in fear.
'I must be brave,'
he thought.

Grrr!

He gripped the stick in his hand, and then threw it with all his strength at the wolf. The stick landed hard on top of its head. With a loud howl, the wolf ran quickly away into the dark forest.

'I've hit it, Kuna!' shouted Gawu happily.

He looked over at his sister but she had fainted.

'Oh, no!' exclaimed Gawu. 'We must get back before the wolf returns.'

Lifting Kuna into his arms, Gawu carried her quickly through the forest.

I must get Kuna home.

Gawu's Idea

That evening, Gawu and his family sat round the fire to eat their supper. Kuna had been asleep most of the day and was now very hungry.

'Pass the bread over, my brave hero,' she said to Gawu.

Gawu's father looked up from his food. 'Why is Gawu a hero?' he asked.

'Didn't Gawu tell you what happened in the forest?' said Kuna in surprise.

'He said that you suddenly fainted,' replied their father.

'But Gawu saved my life!' exclaimed Kuna.

Gawu sighed. He was hoping to keep the rescue a secret. Now his father would start talking about being a warrior.

'Using just a stick, he scared away a large wolf which was about to attack me,' explained Kuna excitedly.

'Well done, Gawu!' said their father proudly. 'You showed the skills of a good Eagle warrior.'

Gawu jumped up angrily. 'I don't want to be an Eagle warrior,' he shouted. 'I want to be a totem pole carver!'

Then he looked at his father nervously. He was in trouble now!

I want to carve!

'To carve the tribe's totem poles is a very important job,' said Gawu's father slowly. 'If you want to be a carver, you will need to show me that you have their special skills. We will talk about it another day. Now we must go and sleep.'

Gawu stayed by the fire as his family went into their hut.

'I must find a way to show Father and Gulas that I can carve a totem pole,' he muttered to himself. 'All I need is a good, strong piece of wood.'

Suddenly he had an idea. Making sure no one was looking, he crept silently back into the dark forest.

The forest seemed very
different at night. It was full of
strange noises and odd shapes.

Gawu crept nervously along the forest path until he came to the place where he had last seen the wolf. Quickly and quietly he looked among the bushes until he found what he was looking for – the long, knobbly stick!

Suddenly there was a loud howl. Grabbing the stick, Gawu ran to the safety of the totem pole workshop.

Sitting near his father's totem pole, Gawu looked at the stick very carefully. He saw how some parts were straight and lined while other parts were curved with circular patterns. The more he looked the more he could see animal faces peering out at him.

Next, Gawu touched the stick. It felt rough and hard in his hands. He let his fingers follow the wood's twists and turns. Gawu drew his ideas in the earth and then, picking up one of Gulas's curved carving knives, he set to work.

The Totem Stick

'Wake up, Gawu. It's morning! What are you doing here?'

Gawu opened his eyes and saw Gulas, the totem pole carver.

'I want to show you something,' Gawu said excitedly. He picked up his stick and handed it nervously to Gulas. It was now a beautifully carved totem pole.

Gulas felt the swirling carved patterns and looked at the four creatures staring out at him. At the top of the stick was a proud eagle.

'Who carved this?' asked Gulas.

'I did,' answered Gawu proudly.

'This is a very good totem pole!' exclaimed Gulas. 'I thought you didn't have the skills yet to be a good carver but you've proved me wrong. Would you still like to work with me?'

'I would love to but I'm not sure my father will let me,' said Gawu sadly.

'Once I show him your carving, I'm sure he will be happy for you to join me,' smiled Gulas.

'Thank you!' said Gawu happily.

He was going to be a totem pole carver at last!

This is a great totem pole!

The Party

Later, at their father's totem pole party, Gawu and Kuna watched as the women from their tribe danced to the beating drums.

Suddenly the drumming and dancing stopped. To the sound of one drum beat, Gulas and a large group of men carried the totem pole to the hole in the ground. They gently slid the bottom of it into the hole and, using ropes, pulled and pushed it up until the pole stood tall and strong before all of the Eagle tribe. Everyone cheered their great warrior.

The chief held up his hand for silence. 'There is still one more totem pole to be put up,' he said. 'Come here, Gawu.'

As Gawu walked up to the chief, he saw his father smiling proudly at him.

There's one more!

The chief held Gawu's small totem pole up high for all the Eagle tribe to see.

'Yesterday, Gawu saved his sister from a wolf. He carved this small totem pole to show what happened.'

The chief pointed at each of the small carved creatures.

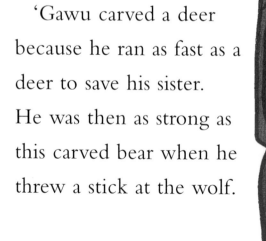

'Gawu carved a deer because he ran as fast as a deer to save his sister. He was then as strong as this carved bear when he threw a stick at the wolf.

'The next is the mink, the animal of friendship. Gawu was a true friend to his sister when he carried her home.

'At the top of the totem pole is the eagle. To be a true Eagle you have to be brave, strong and a good friend to others. Gawu is all of these things.'

He is a true Eagle.

The chief dug a hole in the ground and put the small totem pole in it. 'Now we have two new totem poles to remind us of two special Eagles.'

As the tribe began to dance around the big totem pole, Gawu's father said something to Gawu. He gave his father a big hug and ran happily over to his sister.

'Kuna! Father says I can be a totem pole carver,' said Gawu excitedly.

'Hey, Gawu!'

Gawu looked round and saw the two boys from the day before.

'We were wrong about you, Gawu,' said the big one. 'You are brave.'

'It takes a lot of courage to follow your dream,' said the thin one.

Nice totem pole!

'Thanks,' said Gawu in surprise.

The two boys smiled and began to dance.

Gawu jumped and hopped round and round his totem pole. He was so happy he felt he could dance for ever.

'Gawu, I think you should have carved a rabbit on your totem pole,' said Kuna.

'Why?' he asked.

'Because you dance like one,' she laughed, and she joined in the dance.

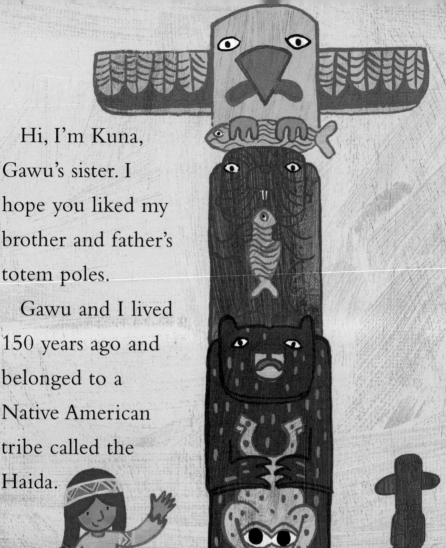

Hi, I'm Kuna, Gawu's sister. I hope you liked my brother and father's totem poles.

Gawu and I lived 150 years ago and belonged to a Native American tribe called the Haida.

Some Haida lived on the Queen Charlotte Islands off the west coast of Canada and were very good totem pole carvers.

Totem poles were also made by other Native American tribes who lived along the northwest coast of the USA and Canada. Today there are only a few totem pole carvers left.

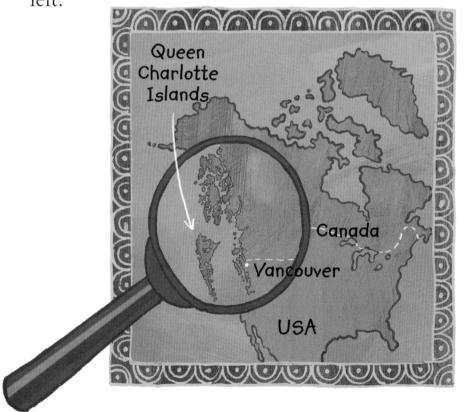

Did you know that the tallest totem pole was thought to be 54.96m (just over 180ft) tall! It was raised in Victoria, Canada in 1994.

That's so big!

Did you know that the thickest totem pole was thought to be 1.8m (6ft) in diameter! It was carved in 1988 in Duncan, Canada.

That's so wide!

All totem poles are carved from the wood of the tall red cedar trees. There are very many red cedar trees where we live. The wood from the tree is very strong and lasts a long time. You can carve wood into many things.

Here is something else that is made from the red cedar tree: a canoe.

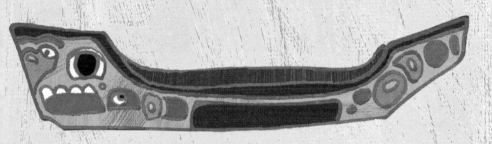

Are there any sculptures or carvings near where you live?

What materials are they made of?

Make your own totem pole!

You'll need to ask an adult to help you with this.

> ## You will need:
> ★ A kitchen towel tube   ★ Two pieces of brown paper
> ★ Scissors   ★ Glue   ★ Crayons   ★ A piece of thick card

How to make it:

1. Wrap one sheet of brown paper around the tube and ask an adult to cut it to fit, allowing some room for overlap.

2. Divide the brown paper into four horizontal sections. Draw a different animal head in the middle of each section and colour them in.

3. Wrap your paper back around the tube and ask an adult to glue the edges down.

4. Draw wings or arms for your animals on the other piece of paper. Ask an adult to cut them out for you and glue them to the back of your totem pole.

5. To make your totem pole stand upright, ask an adult to glue the bottom of your tube onto a piece of thick card.

You have your own totem pole!

What animals did you choose and why?